The Pripet Marshes
and other poems

The Pripet Marshes
and other poems

by Irving Feldman

NEW YORK · THE VIKING PRESS

First published in 1965 by The Viking Press, Inc.
625 Madison Avenue, New York, N.Y. 10022

Published simultaneously in Canada by
The Macmillan Company of Canada Limited

Library of Congress catalog card number: 65-12030
Printed in U.S.A.

"The Pripet Marshes," "Manhattan," and "The Messengers" were first published in *Harper's Bazaar*; "To the Six Million" first appeared in *Midstream*, and "Artist and Model" in *Poetry*; "Portrait de Femme" (I), "Song" (as "Orpheus' Song"), "Scene of a Summer Morning," "Little Lullaby," and "The Double" appeared originally in *The New Yorker*. Some of the other poems were published first in *Columbia University Forum*, *The Literary Review*, *The New York Times*, and *Prism*.

I wish to thank the Ingram Merrill Foundation for enabling me to complete this book.   —I.F.

To Carmen

CONTENTS

The Pripet Marshes
and other poems

PROLOGUE

I in the foreground, in the background I,
And the stone in the center of all,
I by the stone declaiming, I
Writing here, I trundling in
The moody mountain scene, the cardboard
Couples, the dusty star, I turning
From the page, my hand staying moonlit,
My pen athwart the light, I dimming
The moon with cloud, the scene then pensive,
Uneasy, and seated colossal
On the Earth's round brink I, my head bending
My hand back at the wrist, thinking,
Thinking . . . And, still by the stone, I
Attent to my declamation, taking it down.

So the mind above its theater, on
Restless wing aloof, circles
In a thin ether of pain. And I
The more outside holding the global
Thing at arm's length, the sphere withdrawing
Its rounded perfection. Night falling
There, I prompt the little towns to wink,
Show faces sudden at windows, peering
From the radiant blocks; I transmit
The earnest domestic effulgence to
The endless stars, I declare those lives
Indispensable, good, and I think, I think. . . .

The stone, too, floats off, swaying its wide
Circle, taking the all along. I

Bodiless, watching it go, sipping
The transparent pain, the void, sending
My message after it. It goes off,
Gathering the starlight to itself.
And does not shrink. I afterward
Melancholy, such thoughts thinking . . .

THE NURSES

Et vous vous endormez, enfin, dans la blancheur.
　　　　　　　　　　—Henri Calet

Like weary goddesses sick of other worlds—
Those little islands, their drugged white beaches
Where the surf's unending colonies arrive,
And, helpless, the sacrifice lies on altars
Of their indifference, gasping in the sun,
Offering millenniums of his wound—

They, as from the prows of ships stepping,
Come to where the patient worries
The sheet's spreading day, his body
Stilled in drowsy rituals of disaster.
And the marble paradigms, their patient,
Uncaring hands, drop from the salt-parched
Light, gathering your infinite gift,
Its burden.

　　　　　And they whisper,
My prince, my son, relax, forget, give in.
And your memories crowd away into
The gleaming trough, the incurable loss,
Where you dissolve, begin to go off,
Receding, curling away like a wave,
No, like a point. And who will hold you now?
—Falling asleep in the whiteness without end.

Their voices float after you in other worlds,
Other bodies, their hands dwell in your minutest
　　death.

[5]

ARTIST AND MODEL

After Picasso's *Suite de 180 dessins*

I THE ABDUCTION

1

Carefully, he set an easel out,
A page (white), which made the site
A cave, thrusting who had been
Beside him, she, seized, captured, beyond the plane,
Yet not forever into shadow.
On his side, he, O in a motley of loss—chattering
Secretive, sad febrile, sick animal,
Credulous sly, monkey pensive. And she,
Cast away and dormant, lying-in, a model,
Sample, sign pointing mysteriously
From the darkness outward to herself,
What she was, is, still to be, beyond the cave.

II THE SUBJECTION

2 *She*

And not less is, cannot be more,
All center, surface, herself,
Continuous simulacra rising
Outward to this form, what here she is,
Offered in the cave, there flying and glinting
On a hill, spume aloft and facet,
And in the forest there on all
The trees at once dazzled like a wind.

3

And does she think? What thought is possible
To that body's absolute curve, head, its

[6]

Supple repose? Then, if anything,
A rhythm of becomings, herself, her
Innermost, most infinitesimal
Simulacrum in triumph on waves
Of rosiness riding to her skin.
Quickly, this ease he translates
To opportunities, discovers answers,
Landfalls, clues to a something hidden
Where he has left the leavings of his brush
—In armpits and legpit a splotch,
Trickle of hair: three sapient beards.

4 *Monkeyshines*

To his glance opening, teasing
To a gaze nowhere repulsed, never
Satisfied, eludes, confuses him,
She, so and thus, grave, serene.
And he is cross, tracking this endless clue
To a secret that doesn't exist: her
Inside, her other side. And persists, embarks,
Paddling his little cave, sail sighting,
Mozambique, Madagascar, still sail,
Searches under a buttock, along a thigh,
Near ear, dodging among the points
Of view, *Qua qua*, chattering, followed by:
Spoor of anecdotes, vestigia, mask-droppings.

5

He has his way, his trade—and this,
His maker, set its thumbprint on him,
Mark of its power, swirling the lines
Of his face over his smock down the page,
Where his profile's squiggle is justified,
Stayed, in a few satirical dots.

[7]

And she, naked, absolute, posing only
The problem of unity—by which light
He recognizes he is grotesque, perverse,
Embarks on his dialectic, hopping
About in festinate fury, seeking
A slur, a total perspective, to create
Beyond the work her, her garden
Without labor, to repossess that innocence.
Ignorant, she stands. Stymie. On his brow
Finger delves furrow, there between
The worn bumps of horn, warts of thought.

6

He will set her to work. She listens, stares,
Puts on the masks. Why not? the flesh
Accommodates, and welcomes home the wanderer.
All ports are one port; the door opens, the bed's
Page blank. Another mask. Again, here
In the cave where she remains to furnish
The world to her keeper's cell, subjects
For the endless busyness of mind and hand.
Smiling a myopic squint of mouth,
Taking his peek-a-boo of masks for
The gestures of her inwardness, confessions,
Expressions, and lays back her head
For abandon or tilts her elbow for offense.
Upon request, cradles a breast with her hand,
"Like so?" And he, "Hold it!" commands,
Snaps to attention like a thumb.

7

As thought will, his haunts the depths,
Groundswell, the crucible of pressure,
Where the monstrous shape flashes into

[8]

The universe of rhythm. So,
Trawls his net of lines, hunting
The sunken old Venus, the model's other,
Her brine-beaten vestige. And up it comes,
Thumping the cave's keel, enormously
Beyond its calyx reaching, sublime,
Out of the cave, brilliant, defined,
World that, quicker than fish-petal, fin,
Flares piquant in the periscopic eye.

8 *Monkey Art*

The purpose of a line is to create
A transparency, a foreshortening of
The total perspective, that what is not
Seen can be imagined there where it veers
Around and slopes against the backward
Space—of the mind, alas! Imitation
Is magic, abuse of her good kindness
That requires man's sinew, man's breath
To bring (strike! sing!), declare her to herself.
Stuffed with possession, her effigy
Cramping in the perambulator
Of his mind, he strides about,
Refines her to ovoids such and such, hatches them
As schemes that telescope down
To mines of babel. He looks through,
Yes, he sees it, at last! her navel.
Or is it mountains on the moon?

9 *His Monologue*

Cheap tricks, these scribbles and dots,
Data to tick, tickle in mental
IBM: breast, nipples, nose. And these
Polarities, parallels, rhymes,

Dialectics, symmetries; this "like,"
This "stands for"—scum and froth
Of convention, squibble and quibble,
Boundaries of the mind,
Its dark court where fools (two) (Thesis?
Antithesis?) banter a shuttlecock
Across a net and call it phoenix,
Cry, *My* phoenix. Only the court endures,
Persists beyond the badinage of rebirth.
Ground of the mind! Arbitrary lines!
Under the game reclines, out
Of its plane, she, reposing, ungraspable:
Foothold, mountain, sky.

10 *He Speaks of Her Accommodations*

What I have sought, passage outward
Into the garden, where, terror surrendered,
The soul reverts in a shower of seed
—This she presents, dreaming
Salvations, appearances, answering,
At cave's mouth, tower window,
Vocations of hammer, stylus, string,
And shows, in every pose, her happy accident:
Trou: trouvaille, the lucky hole-in-One.

III THE RAPE

11

With passage of the voice, the thing evoked
Drifts back to itself, silence; unblinking
Attention, the note sustained until
It screams, only this can hold it here.
All magic fails, the uneasy metaphor
Of lines collapses; and ancient

Jackanapes must have her all, his feeble
Arms cannot gather her greatness,
Receding, seemingly poised somewhere
Else seemingly beyond flesh.
But now he will enter, deposit his
Inwardness, make her soulful, think,
Swell with pathos, crumble
To characters and roles—and daubs
Her every, her most minute, apparition
With monkey ink.

12   *After*

And, at the last, only ink is, a sea
Of sighs and signs, cave darkness, dark
Petroleum pool whose old metamorphoses
Come, in slow turmoil, surface
Rainbow, surface of fire. Of fire
He thinks, living in a charred moment
After the power, seeking the moment
Before it shined. And makes another
Line, sign: vestige of the power gone,
Pointing a power to come
Where she, regnant, entire, toward herself
Lightly draws him with powerful repose.

BONES FOR THE TOMB OF VIDE

Le meilleur fauxmonnayeur

1

Reader: Leprosy can be
A sort of cosmetology.
Naked bone, the eye its witness,
Yes, indeed, naked man
Is not perhaps, perhaps is
The ultimate in decoration.

Lovely, his glance goes on the glass
Slithering after its remotion
In hymens of self-consciousness.
The terse illustrious skeleton
Shone with such calcium calm
It wanted no art to embalm.

2

Reach, reached, reaching, to reach,
Eye's delighting amorous leech
Fingered the stops of his marrow flute.
Oh for the bliss of a nictitation!
In its swelling embouchure his youth
Was singing, Disincarnation!

Englobed—on the fevered lush floor,
Its fierce grass, its murderous seed,
At the vivid stream, on all fours—
In mind's white paradise, *Vide*,
Inflecting toward his embrace,
Reaches, and drinks a little face.

3

Reader: Also prosthesis
Is a sort of mimesis.
Desire made them, the flesh, the volumes,
The power poised on the flying center.
Ruined, the temple. High columns
Cliché around an empty altar,

Assemble, tremble; manipulation
By crank of iron, clanking brace
Confers facsimiles of consolation
If not gratuities of grace.
Reflected from his rictus-posture,
Vide infers he's feeling pleasure.

4

And otherwise his bones disposes,
After the Grammar of Roles and Poses.
So "If desire flashes and plunges:
With option of tear, leer, or sneer,
Place on one's sternum one's phalanges
To signify 'I am sincere.' "

Though, truly, without desire, or, rather,
Knowing it as something he possessed.
Still, there were the laws of matter,
Motion, gravity, and rest—
It was almost like being in nature,
Before the world had parched to paper.

5

Reader: Was the Mirror,
And Mirror begot the Posture,
And it begot the sterile Now,

Seeing the momentary eye seeing
From the white bewrinkled brow
A brow smoothed to a scruple of being.

And that the stream harried his features,
Broke them to points, flares, divisions,
Convinced him he was many creatures.
Proteus of discrete positions,
The caroling metamorphoses
Halt in his dismal cease.

6

He will not die, neither will he
Destroy, being sterilely
The optimist—of revivisections,
Posterities, new futures,
Pages, paradigms of bones,
And painless gangrenes, clever sutures.

Quite undestroyed, though dead,
Mummied, miraculously slim;
His ghostly banneret of head
Flutters and does not sink or swim.
Flashing, fishing, frothing, fuming, with
    every breath
The river shouts: Assume the power!
    Fulfill the death!

HE

I know him well; and speak as one who knows.
Imagine, then, dear darkened-corner-squatting Ape,
O lifter-of-a-limp-finger-to-furrowed-nose,
Imagine the intemperate scene, and gape.

And first, his humble chasm, and then the day
That stands straight up in parallels to the sky without
Refining shadow or decay, and then the sudden play
Of immense night that whiplike thrashes mountains about,

And these that vaguely crouch like beasts around
The abyss, their fallen prey. There he sits
Before a dressing table, ageless, alone, without a sound,
And mouths into a mirror where his image flits.

But he perseveres among infinities, with whitened wig
And penciled brows; and he can improvise most wittily,
Whatever the lines. Yet time and again, like a moving twig,
He sighs, sighs, sighs extravagantly.

Today he is to be Voltaire, but they will not cue,
Or if they call he will not hear; and the mirror trembles like
    a veil
And the mountains creep near. And then he says like you,
Imagine it! he *says* he is *not* the Devil!

"PORTRAIT DE FEMME"

After Picasso

I

Somewhere between our nervousness and
Our admiration, she sits in her portrait
—Une femme, with two noses, in a striped blouse,
Being poked fun at, feeling doubtless
Herself honored by this satirist so famous
No one laughs any more, she, the chosen
One, of flippered arms and perfunctory fingers,
A visage clawed in colors, one heartless
Breast a blank circle, on her vase-stem
Neck imposed, a brow like Gibraltar's.
Maybe it is Dora Maar—"charming, talented,
Vivacious"—composed here on a collapsing
Chair between three jokes (on the flesh,
On vanity, on painting)—whose iron mouth
And clear fixated gaze betray to all
The world only the fiercest equanimity.

II THE ONE VERITY

Flesh is what, exactly? And the spirit—"witty,
Vivacious, provocative"—livening it,
What? Mysteries rendered negotiable by
A sly counterfeiter who's countersigned her Maar,
Merely, having, ungently, reinvented her all
—One lady, in one chair—and cashed her in
For the small change of relation, except:
The imagined horizontal connecting to one eye
Corner the next. The rest is paint.
Behind the eyes on the goblet-head, defined
By the jest of unkiltered metamorphoses, is:

A liquid just level, precariously still. This
Not to spill a life long while providing witty
Vivacity with vivacious provocation—this
Is perhaps the soul and quite enough
To make dear Psyche weary, bright Eros weep.

III WHO IS DORA? WHAT IS SHE?

Perhaps on such a day as this—but
In France in 1936, before,
That is, the War and other events
Now too infinite to list (though
Out-of-doors the oak whispers not
And the birds exist much as
They did and will) came and went
Like that and like this, all things
That time bore and then dismissed
—Before the War perhaps, on such
A day as this, Dora Maar (let us
Say, "Dora Maar," for who would be
Anonymous? and her name was all
She really wore) sat in a chair
In 19 and 36 with a wish fierce
And commonplace to be mysterious,
To survive and to thrive, to be a success
And be good, and be covered
With paint like a kiss,
Eternally, in nineteen hundred thirty-six.

IN TIME OF TROUBLES

In time of trouble, prophets
Abound: excrement of stone,
Rushing from hallways, ardent
And spastic in the spotlight of their aura.
Mumming children yowl on the street,
Women in aprons follow after
Wailing, the dinner's turnip
And paring knife waved in their hands
And the half-mad feel the key wince round,
Released from their hutches, bolt out
Into the street, direct the traffic.
Around the prophets all hunch, hushed
To hear the headline scale the sheer walls
Of their throats: "Gr-r-eat-est!" It is the circus
Of pestilence. Convulsed, gurgling,
The murderous martyrs drop
Away to their holy pratfalls.
Void next: sudden of the streetcorner:
Where machine guns connect
With a wicked wisecrack.
The crowd like cards fanned, flying.
On high bridges and high buildings
Vague figures lean, leap out
Over the treetops. The looters, however,
Do not observe the holiday,
Keep their wits,
Quietly
From door to door . . .

THE FALSE ONE

It was he, the False One, opened the door
When I stretched my hand, led me on, whisking
The corridor under my feet, covered
My enemy in flickering mists
And hid him away, then brought me out to
The street. And again hid him among crowds,
And, touching lightly the gas, brought me
By stages of green light easy from the city
To the dry grasses, the merciless quarry,
Where again I sought him, my adversary.
Undaunted, he came forward, and I leaned
To him. Nothing. Mirage of the False One.
Possessed, I was falling, fell through air,
My fit flailing in me, battering ribs,
Grappling my lung. And I prayed, falling, God,
Destroy the False One, and, as before,
Give me my enemy into my power!

LIGHT

Some things catch the light
A moment, or more, some
It passes by. Here and there
Men appear, blind, illuminated,
In a city somewhere, say,
Receiving light like a grace
One certain day. In darkness
Disappear. Blessed is sight, blest
That here and there, beyond
The fabling mind, its failings
In the dark, men appear
Before they go away.

DARK NIGHTS

ONE

What woke you? waking
At night, starved for seeing,
Invisible, blind? It takes
You then in disavowals,
Rhetoric of belly blows,
Heart gougings, persuades you
Of the dark, the nullity,
The taking away.
Dittos of the watch.
You cannot think, wakened
At night, starving,
How the day will come,
Fullness of the sun.

TWO

If night; if nothing appear,
All else at secret rest,
You in room, waked
By heart's bone, night
Blows you out, blind, invisible,
Nothing if nothing appear.
If nothing, night, dissolved
In untouchable black,
You cannot cry out, wordless
Till the light.

THREE

When they laughed at you
And made the night uproarious,
Waking, you joined the mockers

—Catcurse, dogdank,
The great shame-man—
And laughed down at him there,
Much worse than the others,
Laughing, pointing the finger,
Denying, decrying.
But when the light possessed him
And he was again himself,
You were left alone on the ceiling,
Possessing nothing, not a thing,
Ignorant little devil.

FOUR

The night, it woke you, fingered
You, took the string
And led you on, toy
Of that ancient child, tugged
By him around the room,
And squeak went your wood wheels,
Whinnies of laughter, too.
Oh, for the ancient night journey
Through the chill famished spaces,
A real wooden wagon,
Empty, and taken away
On round wooden wheels
That went turning, oh, not yourself,
Believe that! or anyone else,
But a wagon, a real
Wooden wagon gone gaily,
Quite gaily away! with the night.

FIVE

Let there be light! You wanted
To say that, but you who must,
Doing, undo, unmake,

You, have you something
To offer? The night, too,
Did not want you as you were,
Or, transformed, another.
In its black lung, burning,
You warm the thing you could
Not be. Vast, illimitable,
The night of denials,
Over, over it turns
In the faceless deep. Rise,
Rise, bright renegade,
Having made the night
Greater, make the day!

LITTLE LULLABY

Dark-time. The little ones like bees
Have stolen the light, packed it away
In their healthy mandibles and gone off.
Rest, little soul, of your lithe cunnings,
Of your tattling tattoo undressed. They
Have taken the daylight in their keeping;
Safe in the hive, hidden, it will not chide
You if you are silent. At last, listen:
Under the fallow sad song of your neighbor's
Life, or the blood waltzing in your ear:
Dispossessed, uncharming, enormous
Bodies approach; they wish to fulfill you.

MANHATTAN

In memory of Adelle Goldberg Irving (1928–1957)
The memory of the righteous is a blessing.

I

Unlike most hearts known to me,
Money is, in the style of the gods,
Happy, has no anxiety,
Does not idle, despair, fear
The bomb, smiles from gay façades
Its nicer triumphs of increment.
Yes, they go on building here,
The city's unending! great holes
Where the shovel's dripping instrument
Gorges by the distant shoring,
The rain is drowned in trampled shoals.
Passers-by, drawn bodiless
Down by the raw dark nothing
Of it, dream with infatuate art
Dim silent lives and blest
Returns. Trucks take it away,
The fill of useless city dirt,
The shapeless dun gravities
Of a sweeter land. I, too, delay—
For another life, recall that twilight
To this clay, its windblown bright seeds,
Light gardens of the air!
And works when first my little might
Summoned Dog or Cat (from where?)
To a blue embodiment there.
No doubt (no doubt! my rising ghost
Agrees), to build into the air
Is good, catch and delight the eye
And herald back the body lost

With that astonishing counterpart
—Shape in the street against the sky
That brings the body to bear. This, best,
Fulfillment for the laboring heart
And in the heart of labor, rest.

II

Glass, steel, stone paste,
Surely, a building will annul
The dim vacancy of this waste,
Where, this day, my ghost is still,

Waiting between the graveyard brood
Of floors, the city's lost lair,
And the unredeemed promise renewed
In the empty unconceivable air,

While, dispirited, my body pauses,
Abstracted, vague, goes—gowned
In its zone of distance, losses,
In all the superb absence drowned—

Dispersed between the nothing before,
Nothing hereafter, to wait,
At drizzling dusk in the stifled splendor,
Timeless that nothing abide, abate,

Blind mantis at the empty grave,
Invoking blankness it foresees;
Prospective ruins in me revive
As lapsings of my memories.

It will be dark again. Desire,
Was it you dazzling in the air
The ancient promise? the pillar of fire?
Toward a sweeter land not here?

Will be dark. Secret, supernal, vast,
Over the street's effigy,
A distant body inspires the last
Brilliance from the alien debris.

III

Half-night now. And the drover
Twilight drives them out,
Home from the darkened office
And glaring shop, on their brows
The sootfall's satiric loam,
The ceaseless downward drizzle,
The neon's sour cosmetic.
God knows! it's time to go,
Get away from this,
And join them underground.
Rock among the streamfaces,
I stay, for sweetness' sake,
And for your memory's sake, I wait,
So, concentrated, waiting,
A body can pray, can summon
Every abandoned ghost
However hard the clay.

Sweetness, cousin, sweet water,
Won't you come a little way here?
Out of the earth and out of the water?
Into the street at stunning twilight
Here while I wait and stay?
Now gone from the grave, good news!
Do you meander on below
In the festive first city?
—Atlantis-ghetto washed clean
Where all is brightened, scoured, mended,

Renewed for the heart's sabbath eve!
And the gentle pigeon-breasted women
Of our line go together at ease,
Bearing candles in our memory
And singing for us under the sea.

Blazing, the empty carnival here,
The buildings empty, the street,
Yet, below, the darkness roars
Where, dispossessed, they go,
Restless, pastless, home,
Bringing themselves in their arms,
Trinkets from the burning
Toyshop hauled, the china
Women, chalk men, like lares
Of the ended fair.

Are you, too, a ghost, my dear?,
Homeward in a lilac dress, hair
Caught back, your cheeks ruddy,
Eyes lit with a newer,
Gentler victory, and prattling
With woman's kindliness,
A child's vivacity,
Most marvelous things?
Won't you, rising toward the streetlamps'
Old lucre, bring the city-seed,
Sweetness, cousin, and restore
The memory? ripened block
Of Atlantic marble, the sabbath-stone
With its water-flame and water-glow . . .
And who alone shall see you, sweetness,
Cousin, child arrived—it is I!
All prosper with the sweeter land!

POEM AT THIRTY-FIVE

Many smile, but few are happy; my friends,
Their lives hardening about them, are stern
With misery, knowing too well their ends.
—But are these destinies, or mock-destinies,
Or both at once? They will answer as they please.
But a spring day arrives at them like a knife.
And they *want* to break out, but that day, too,
Is so hard—yet bravely (for all are brave)
They press against it (and it hurts, be sure); their might
Is all in that, unbroken where the airs move against
Them; they are drawn down to that point. And here the
    night
Finds them, harder, testing their strength, tensed.

Despair brutalizes. That is the law. (But
Is there music in that?) My friends, feeling
Their lives hardening, grow harder, less appealing;
Almost the past condoning, almost a pleasure
Finding there they cannot in their harder future,
Though they know, as we say, the two go together.
So wise men have said all things return.

(Many smile, but few are happy; my friends,
With misery, knowing too well their ends,
Their lives hardening about them, are stern.)

FORGIVING ADAM

Adam in the garden; plainly now
I see him in the fruitful light
Moving, carrying the light, his bright
Eyes making bright the garden bough.

I too am in a garden, which is not
Other than my life—here tawdry,
However, or gray and boring with something
Not unlike death, though, surely, not,

Despite its hidden dim display,
Different much from Adam's garden,
For here too is light, if I pardon.
Will not this grayness drift away,
The gaudy night grow plain, if I can
Forgive Adam? forgive the man
I was who made the garden gray.

THE NO-NIGHT

It was the night of hardly anyone,
And you, among the nobodies
Disguised there, nothing yourself.

One figure two-hoofed it in donkey-fleece
With head yawing no, his eyes
Rolling wide, hideous.

And you watched titillated, scandalized,
Too, by the mock-gypsy, the mirrors-
Man, nothing yourself.

Vulgarity, ineptness of their gestures
(And the monkey-magus, the catcurd)
Showed their void-fear fever

As shadows galloped, stumbled away, staggered;
Toward midnight the hysteria froze.
You heard, nothing yourself,

The "Let-me-out-of-my-life!" of their cackle news,
Beholding the spastic tableau
Of midnight zero until

"Let me out of my life!" you madly echo
The toad-throats, the not-nothing masks,
Then nothing yourself

Among the shattering blank icicle-tusks,
The dead disguises puddled
Under the great dawn,

You gone too, nothing yourself.

[31]

THE MESSENGERS

To those (only to those?)
Who abandon all, yes,
To the great abandoners
Unliving their lives all,
The ecstatic messengers come
Unconscious of their tunics'
Heartbreaking expressive fall,
Their gusty disheveled curls,
Their cheeks puffing as if
One second more they will
Lift their trumpets and call.

Radiant, they, and always
Earliest arriving
To precede the lavish day
Like the light prophesying
At dawn, lighting nothing
For nothing yet is born,
They are almost turning
To go, almost are gone,
Already spoken the word
Delightfully their faces shine,
And fullness of the day
In a blaze of trumpet metal:

See how I love my life!
Faithless,
You have loved your lives too little.

TO LUCIFER

You to the infinite dawn recalled
From the eclipse and the end of things,
The looming mote of broken playthings
Only your dusty eyelids recalled,

And your life that was your exile; recalled
At last to the empty place of light
And ecstasy of the half-light
Sweeping superb by no thing recalled

From the infinite dawn—you arise,
Light renegade, recalling to the day
The lights of the long yesterday
And next days now singular in the skies

With you to the infinite dawn.

THE DOUBLE

On other cloudy afternoons
You will be sitting here, or pacing
The rooms, your restless words
Unuttered. I put you there now
So the drama may continue, with poplars
Invoking the wind outside, the lamplight
Slowly focusing to a pencil point.
Here, it is murdering an angel
In the very center of everywhere. This same
Joy shall be yours, drawing the blood out
Among these mazes that continue
Always, under the aspects
Of a cloudy day.
                    Mysterious the mazes
Of those afternoons through which
The red leaves sweep, your own hand
Tracing joyfully there another life
To live you on afternoons like this.

SCENE OF A SUMMER MORNING

Scene of a summer morning, my mother walking
To the butcher's, I led along. Mountains
Of feathers. My breath storms them. Angry feathers.
Handfuls. The warm gut windings stinking.
Here, chickens! Yankel, the bloody storeman,
Daringly he takes the live animals
In vain. Yankel, a life for a life! Eternal
Morning too young to go to school. I get
A hollow horn to keep. Feathers, come down!
Gone. The world of one morning. But somewhere,
Sparkling, it circles a sunny point.

Incredible the mazes of that morning,
Where my life in all the passages at once
Is flowing, coursing, as in a body
That walked away, went.
                              Who writes these lines
I no longer know, but I believe him
To be a coward, that only one who escaped.
The best and bravest are back there still,
All my Ten Tribes wandering and singing
In the luminous streets of the morning.
Unsounded the horn! And silence shudders
In the center of the sunny point,
Heartstopping at dawn.
Enormous my thieving hand in the ancient sunlight
No longer mine. Littering through my fingers,
Drifting, the Ten Tribes there, gone forever.

CLOWN AND DESTINY

And you improvise; yet there is always
The dead one among the shifting figures,
The old knight in his armor fallen
On the stifled ground. And still you continue:
Being dog, or starlight, or turning ocean,
Yet return always to the one figure
Lying hinted among the silences
(Starry spur, helmet on a tossing sea).
Evolving at length among the renewals
Of your painted face (the goat, the ruined
Columns, starlight, and turning ocean),
The constellation of most ancient light:
The dead one enormous in armor, sworn.
And after the turning ocean, or starlight,
Or man imperiled, you become the dead one,
Standing, hefting the halberd, departing
Again into the salt-stung wilderness,
Where the wave goes under and you wander
Armored to battle what killing thing appears:
Starlight or dog or turning ocean.

THE NEW NIGHT

When the night arrived supreme
Over the empty place,
Safe in death hiding,
You went on denying,
But, Let there be light! said
Your eyes with desire,
And there *was* light,
Light without color,
And the new night was newer.

Will the night arrive, asked
Your tongue, that I may greet it?
And the little light was there,
Bespoken and a danger,
Very little
And a star,
And the new night was newer.

Has the night come? said
Your body, I wish to arise.
And you arose,
A little way,
And were the light
And the danger,
Little light without color.
And the new night was newer.

THE RETURN

Was this life? Good, let it come again!
—Nietzsche

Did you speak those words?
But if your life were given you again . . .
—But as another turning of the maze,
Or the same maze a second time;
And not the struggle you wanted,
But intricate escaping whispers
That hint (or simulate) a mystery,
And bring you (your enemy retreating,
Scattered among lurkings, absences)
Toward a struggle deflected
Through minute, imperative clashes,
Till, circling on the infinite threshold,
Your weariness and your way unite;
Past, future connect in a dream
That there is no adversary, no ending . . .

Yet suppose that on this
Your own occluded morning
(With the wind idly revolving,
The rain oppressing the streets
With impetuous disdainful imminence),
Suppose that over and over
Your life returns,
Mingling in a radiant moment
Those turnings, those doorways, and days,
Your mumbled streets of mazes
Flashing out in the singular falls!
But you, perplexed in the roaring
Of the simultaneous syllable,

Go blind,
   unable to recall
The name of life
    —as this day
(On your own cloudy morning,
The wind idling, turning,
The rain above the streets withheld)
You turn,
Under the momentous, pouring body,
And search the doubtful passageways
(Repeated, dividing), unaware
That from the first your cry was answered,
And your life, and lives, are here.

NIGHTWORDS

Sitting alone, I cannot write.
There is someone missing.
Or many are missing.
Still, I am happy to sit at these words
And think of you lying
In another room, where your sleep
Is all my power over you,
Wanting, though I do not, to wake you,
To ask, Does music sleep, too?
Are you the sleeping music?

My questions are furtive,
I do not inquire aloud
For the sake of companioning sound,
For the music is sleeping with faint
Subterranean breathings if I listen,
My century of fathers and sons,
Enchanted dynasty in a farther cell,
Where you are lying asleep
As if in a leisure
I perhaps am feigning.
How deep is that dungeon! how
Far from me! where your breaths,
So many, like letters are setting out
To seek no other destination.
When you sleep, I dream
I am the assassin-king
Banished from your green country,

But are you in heaven in that other room?
If you were waking, approaching . . .

But you sleep again your own sleep,
And alone I survive into the moment,
Sitting here, waiting for the music
To revive, arrive,
And the night to grow new.
I cannot think of anything
Without thinking of you,
No, not a word without the music!
And dream I have gone to visit, to bend
Over you—(my furtive questions,
Thieves in the clouded room,
Have they stolen your waking?
This barren lime of my eyes ablaze,
Blinded, intense?)—and bend over you
And listen to my attentive hearing, dark sky
Into which your breath is flying
From drowsy exile with a sound of voices.
That might be the great restoring music . . .
To the graves of our dearest victims
We cast: our loveliest flowers.
And they seem to take root there, to thrive.
But I will not elegize, for you sleep
Merely, immortally, no death
Can be committed, though you are
Elsewhere in the other room
Perhaps, sleeping I think,
And dream me as I am? wakeful, confused?
I no longer know which side
Of your sleep's disguise is mine,
Or who we are.

But I am trying to write a poem,
I have set myself to this task,

That is how close we come,
Toward this clearing, this needle eye,
I and the sleeping music, two breaths
In the situation, turning toward
Each other with a slight difference
Each time. I am trying,
Listening in a field where I and your breath
May meet in an instant.

The poem is in the center, but
In the center of the poem
Is emptiness.
Yet the moment develops,
From my sitting here, your sleep, my effort, my
    waiting,
Pairing the dancers for the promenade
On the endless roads
Around the sunny point,
The voice in the light,
Involving the arabesque I
And your breaths are playing, hunting
Each other toward the clearing, weaving
The little leaf anew, the same leaf
Bearing two dangers on its greener side,
Two breaths.
I do not ask questions aloud,
Scrupulous in exile,
I do not wake you.
But from your other room
You come toward the poem
I am trying to write in a pitiless moment,
Making my blind attentive sky
That invites your breath to come flying

In the needle eye
With a voice of restoration . . . dreaming,

Dreamt, sitting alone,
Waiting, trying, for the music
To revive, arrive,
And the night to grow new.

Often I think of my Jewish friends and seize them as they
are and transport them in my mind to the *shtetlach* and
ghettos,

And set them walking the streets, visiting, praying in *shul*,
feasting and dancing. The men I set to arguing, because
I love dialectic and song—my ears tingle when I hear their
voices—and the girls and women I set to promenading or
to cooking in the kitchens, for the sake of their tiny feet
and clever hands.

And put kerchiefs and long dresses on them, and some of
the men I dress in black and reward with beards. And all
of them I set among the mists of the Pripet Marshes,
which I have never seen, among wooden buildings that
loom up suddenly one at a time, because I have only
heard of them in stories, and that long ago.

It is the moment before the Germans will arrive.

Maury is there, uncomfortable, and pigeon-toed, his voice
is rapid and slurred, and he is brilliant;
And Frank who is goodhearted and has the hair and yellow
skin of a Tartar and is like a flame turned low;
And blonde Lottie who is coarse and miserable, her full
mouth is turning down with a self-contempt she can
never hide, while the steamroller of her voice flattens
every delicacy;
And Marian, her long body, her face pale under her bewil-
dered black hair and of the purest oval of those Greek

signets she loves; her head tilts now like the heads of the
birds she draws;

And Adele who is sullen and an orphan and so like a beaten
creature she trusts no one, and who doesn't know what to
do with herself, lurching with her magnificent body like
a despoiled tigress;

And Munji, moping melancholy clown, arms too short for
his barrel chest, his penny-whistle nose, and mocking
nearsighted eyes that want to be straightforward and
good;

And Abbie who, when I listen closely, is speaking to me,
beautiful with her large nose and witty mouth, her color-
ing that always wants lavender, her vitality that body and
mind can't quite master;

And my mother whose gray eyes are touched with yellow,
and who is as merry as a young girl;

And my brown-eyed son who is glowing like a messenger
impatient to be gone and who may stand for me.

I cannot breathe when I think of him there.

And my red-haired sisters, and all my family, our embar-
rassed love bantering our tenderness away.

Others, others, in crowds filling the town on a day I have
made sunny for them; the streets are warm and they are
at their ease.

How clearly I see them all now, how miraculously we are
linked! And sometimes I make them speak Yiddish in
timbres whose unfamiliarity thrills me.

But in a moment the Germans will come.

What, will Maury die? Will Marian die?

Not a one of them who is not transfigured then!

[45]

The brilliant in mind have bodies that glimmer with a
    total dialectic;
The stupid suffer an inward illumination; their stupidity
    is a subtle tenderness that glows in and around them;
The sullen are surrounded with great tortured shadows rag-
    ing with pain, against whom they struggle like titans;
In Frank's low flame I discover an enormous perspectiveless
    depth;
The gray of my mother's eyes dazzles me with our love;
No one is more beautiful than my red-haired sisters.
And always I imagine the least among them last, one I did
    not love, who was almost a stranger to me.
I can barely see her blond hair under the kerchief; her
    cheeks are large and faintly pitted, her raucous laugh
    is tinged with shame as it subsides; her bravado forces
    her into still another lie;
But her vulgarity is touched with a humanity I cannot ex-
    haust, her wretched self-hatred is as radiant as the faith
    of Abraham, or indistinguishable from that faith.
I can never believe my eyes when this happens, and I want
    to kiss her hand, to exchange a blessing

In the moment when the Germans are beginning to enter
    the town.

But there isn't a second to lose, I snatch them all back,
For, when I want to, I can be a God.
No, the Germans won't have one of them!
This is my people, they are mine!

And I flee with them, crowd out with them; I hide myself
    in a pillowcase stuffed with clothing, in a woman's knot-
    ted handkerchief, in a shoebox.

And one by one I cover them in mist, I take them out.
The German motorcycles zoom through the town,
They break their fists on the hollow doors.
But I can't hold out any longer. My mind clouds over.
I sink down as though drunk or beaten.

TO THE SIX MILLION

*But put forth thine hand now, and
touch his bones and his flesh . . .*

I

If there is a god,
He descends from the power.
But who is the god rising from death?
(So, thunder invades the room, and brings with it
A treble, chilly and intimate, of panes rattling
On a cloudy day in winter.
But when I look through the window,
A sudden blaze of sun is in the streets,
Which are, however, empty and still. The thunder
Repeats.) Thunder here. The emptiness resounds
Here on the gods' struggle-ground
Where the infinite negative retreats,
Annihilating where it runs,
And the god who must possess pursues, pressing
On window panes, passing through.
Nothing's in the room but light
Wavering beneath the lamp
Like a frosty rose the winter bled.
No one is in the room (I possess nothing),
Only power pursuing, trying
Corpses where the other god went,
Running quickly below the door. In
The chill, the empty room
Reverberates. I look from the window.

———

There is someone missing.
Is it I who am missing?

And many are missing.
And outside, the frozen street extends
From me like a string, divides, circles,
Returns, retreats, uncanny
And perpetual with an emptiness the sun
Is burnishing. Gathers, cancels, annuls
Every glance, mere place
Where no one is, no footstep,
No voice but thunder
Repeating, approaching, demurring.
What does not end, fractions, repeats;
Persisting, the changeless articulates
As a maze infinitely that, suddenly,
Has collapsed to a white spore
Floating on a tiny string.
                              In the street
There is nothing, for many are missing,
Or there is the death of the many
Missing, annulled, dispossessed,
Filling the street, pressing their vacancy
Against the walls, the sunlight, the thunder.
Is a god
In the street? where nothing is left
To possess, nothing to kill;
And I am standing
Dead at the window looking out.

———

What did you kill? Whom did you save? I ask
Myself aloud, clinging to the window
Of a winter day.
                      Survivor, who are you?
Ask the voices that disappeared,
The faces broken and expunged.

I am the one who was not there.
Of such accidents I have made my death.

Should I have been with them
On other winter days in the snow
Of the camps and ghettos?
And when the fire anointed them,
And on the days of their death that was
The acrid Polish air?—
I who lay between the mountain of myrrh
And the hill of frankincense,
Dead and surviving, and dared not breathe.
And asked, By what right am I myself?
(But long before, and after a little sleep,
In a stifled room I had awakened,
Quiescent between the flickering cycles
Of killing and saving.)

Who I am I do not know,
But I believe myself to be one
Who should have died, and the dead one
Who did die.
                    When I wake again
I am my dead brother (and I am you),
Stillborn from the barren streets.
Here on the struggle-ground, impostor
Of a death, I survive reviving,
Perpetuating the accident;
I have not lived, he has not died.
And who is at the window pane,
Clinging, lifting himself like a child
To the scene of a snowless day?

———

"Whatsoever is under the whole heaven
Is mine." Charred, abandoned, all this,
Who will call these things his own?

Who died not
To be dying, to survive
My death dead as I am
At the window (possessing nothing),
And died not to know
The agony of the absence,
Reviving on a day
When thunder rattles the panes,
Possessed by no one;
Bone and flesh of me, because
You died on other days
Of actual snow and sun,
Under mists and chronic rain,
My death is cut to the bone,
My survival torn from me.
I would cover my nakedness
In dust and ashes. They, too, burn,
They are hot to the touch. Can such
Death live? The chill treble
Squeaks for a bone. I was
As a point in a space,
By what right can I be myself?
At the window and in the streets,
Among the roots of barbed wire,
And by springs of the sea,
To be dying my death again
And with you,
In the womb of ice, and where
The necessity of our lives is hid.
Bone and flesh of me,

[51]

I have not survived,
I would praise the skies,
Leap to the treasures of snow.

II

> *By night on my bed I sought him whom my soul*
> *loveth: I sought him, but I found him not.*
>
> *I will rise now, and go about the city in the streets,*
> *and in the broad ways I will seek him whom my*
> *soul loveth . . .*

What can I say?
               Dear ones, what can I say?
You died, and emptied the streets
And my breath, and went from my seeing.
And I awoke, dying at the window
Of my wedding day, because
I was nowhere; the morning that revived
Was pain, and my life that began again was pain,
I could not see you.
                  What can I say?
My helpless love overwhelmed me,
Sometimes I thought I touched your faces,
My blindness sought your brows again,
And your necks that are towers,
Your temples that are as pieces
Of pomegranate within your locks.
Dead and alive,
Your shadows escaped me. I went
Into the streets, you were not there,
For you were murdered and befouled.
And I sought you in the city,
Which was empty, and I found you not,
For you were bleeding at the dayspring

[52]

And in the air. That emptiness
Mingled with my heart's emptiness,
And was at home there, my heart
That wished to bear you again, and bore
The agony of its labor, the pain
Of our birth. And I sought for you
About the city in the streets, armed
With the love hundreds had borne me.
And before the melancholy in the mazes,
And the emptiness in the streets,
In the instant before our deaths,
I heard the air (that was
To be ashen) and the flesh
(That was to be broken), I heard
Cry out, Possess me!
And I found you whom my soul loves;
I held you, and would not let you go
Until I had brought you
Into my mother's house, and into the chamber
Of her that conceived me.

Dear ones, what can I say?
I must possess you no matter how,
Father you, befriend you,
And bring you to the lighthearted dance
Beside the treasures and the springs,
And be your brother and your son.
Sweetness, my soul's bride,
Come to the feast I have made,
My bone and my flesh of me,
Broken and touched,
Come in your widow's raiment of dust and ashes,
Bereaved, newborn, gasping for
The breath that was torn from you,

That is returned to you.
There will I take your hand
And lead you under the awning,
And speak the words it behooves to speak.
My heart is full, only the speech
Of the ritual can express it.
And after a little while,
I will rouse you from your dawn sleep
And accompany you in the streets.

SONG

So you are

Stone, stone or star,
Flower, seed,
Standing reed,
River going far

So you are

Shy bear or boar,
Huntsman, death,
Arising breath,
Stone, stone or star

So you are.